Tinker Bell Tales

Little, Brown and Company

Hachette Book Group
1290 Avenue of the Americas, New York, NY 10104
Visit us at lb-kids.com

Little, Brown and Company is a division of Hachette Book Group, Inc.
The Little, Brown name and logo are trademarks of Hachette Book Group, Inc.

The publisher is not responsible for websites (or their content)
that are not owned by the publisher.

First Edition: November 2015
Meet Tinker Bell originally published in 2008 by Random House Children's Books
Meet Tinker Bell previously published in 2014 by Little, Brown and Company
Meet Periwinkle originally published in 2012 by Random House Children's Books
Meet Periwinkle previously published in 2014 by Little, Brown and Company
Meet Rosetta and *Meet Silvermist* originally published in 2015 by Little, Brown and Company

ISBN 978-0-316-35269-7

10 9 8 7 6 5 4 3 2

APS

Printed in China

Passport to Reading titles are leveled by independent reviewers applying the
standards developed by Irene Fountas and Gay Su Pinnell in *Matching Books
to Readers: Using Leveled Books in Guided Reading*, Heinemann, 1999.

Tinker Bell Tales

L B

LITTLE, BROWN AND COMPANY
New York · Boston

Table of Contents

Meet Tinker Bell

By Apple Jordan

Illustrated by the Disney Storybook Art Team

Attention, Disney Fairies fans!
Look for these words when you read
this story. Can you spot them all?

Silvermist

fireflies

owl

mouse

It is a big day for the fairies
who live in Pixie Hollow.

A new fairy is born.

Her name is Tinker Bell.

Queen Clarion tells Tinker Bell

she is born of laughter,

clothed in cheer,

and that happiness brought her here.

Each fairy has a talent.

What is Tinker Bell's talent?

The fairies give her light,

water, and flowers.

Nothing happens.

The fairies give Tinker Bell a hammer.

It glows.

Tinker Bell has found her talent!

She is a tinker fairy.

Tinkers fix things.

The other tinker fairies
welcome Tinker Bell.

Bobble and Clank show her
Pixie Hollow.

Then Tinker Bell meets Fairy Mary.

Fairy Mary is the head tinker.

"Being a tinker stinks,"
Tinker Bell tells Fairy Mary.
Tinker Bell wants to try
other talents.

Silvermist is a water fairy.

But Tink is not good with water.

She makes a splash.

Tink tries to be a light fairy.

The fireflies chase her away.

Tinker Bell tries to be an animal fairy.

She wants to help the baby owl.

But she scares the owl.

Tinker Bell keeps trying.

She tries to ride

Cheese the mouse.

Tinker Bell and Cheese
crash into the gate.

It opens.

All the Thistles run out.

The fairies are getting ready

for the spring season.

The Thistles run this way and that.

They run over the berries and seeds

for spring.

Tinker Bell made this mess.

Queen Clarion is upset.

How will they get ready

for spring now?

Tinker Bell has an idea.

She asks Bobble and Clank for help.

They make tools to make new things
for spring.

Tinker Bell saves spring
using her tinker talent.
All the fairies are happy.
The happiest fairy is
Queen Clarion.

Tinker Bell is happy.
She is a tinker fairy
and proud of it!

Meet Periwinkle

Adapted by Celeste Sisler

Tinker Bell and Fairy Mary
are making baskets.

Each owl takes one basket
to the Winter Woods.
Frost fairies use them
to collect snowflakes.

Warm fairies cannot go
to the Winter Woods.
The cold hurts their wings.
Tinker Bell is curious.

She looks on with Fawn as
the animals get ready to
cross into the Winter Woods.

Tink wants to learn more.
She goes to the library
and takes out a book by
the Keeper.

The next day, Tink

goes to find the Keeper.

The Keeper is in

the Winter Woods.

She hides in a basket

and flies away.

Tink lands in the Winter Woods.

She hides behind the basket.

Her book falls out.

The ruler of the Winter Woods
sees it and gets mad.
"Return this book
to the Keeper," he tells a fairy.
Tink follows the fairy!

The fairy leads Tink
to the Hall of Winter.
The Keeper and
a frost fairy are there.
The frost fairy's name
is Periwinkle.

Their wings start to

sparkle and shine.

Tink and Peri fly

near each other.

The Keeper smiles.

The Keeper takes Tink and Peri

to a special room.

He shows them their past.

The two fairies were born
of the same laugh,
and then it split in two.
Tink and Peri are sisters!

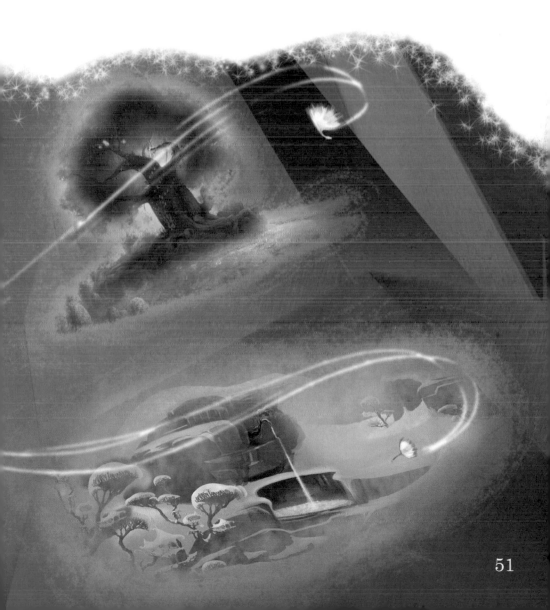

They are so happy!

Periwinkle takes Tink sledding.

She shows Tink her Found Things.

They build a fire
together, too.

Soon, Tink has to go home.

The sisters hug good-bye.

Peri wants to visit Pixie Hollow.

Tink and her friends build a
snow machine.

They hope it will help Peri stay cold.

Bobble and Clank help
Tinker Bell bring the
machine to the border
of Pixie Hollow.
Peri is there.

Periwinkle flies up
to the machine.
Snowflakes encircle
her wings.

The snow machine works.

Peri's wings are safe!

Periwinkle meets all of
Tink's friends and shows
them her frost talent.
It makes the fairies smile.

But soon it gets warmer.

Periwinkle's wings start to fall.

She needs to fly back to

the Winter Woods.

Suddenly, the snow machine
slides into a waterfall.
It gets stuck!

It turns on and
starts making snow.
Pixie Hollow begins
to freeze!

Tinker Bell asks Peri for
help from the frost fairies.
"Their frost can protect the tree,"
Tink explains to Fairy Mary
and the queen.

The frost fairies arrive and
get to work right away.

The frost fairies freeze
the Pixie Dust Tree.
The sun comes out and
melts the frost.
The tree starts making
dust again!

Thanks to Periwinkle
and the frost fairies,
Pixie Hollow is saved!
Everyone is happy.

Meet
Rosetta

By Celeste Sisler

Attention, Disney Fairies fans!
Look for these words when you read
this story. Can you spot them all?

flowers

dress

feather

garden

Rosetta is a garden-talent fairy.

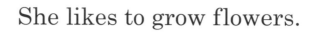

She likes to grow flowers.

Rosetta plays dress-up in her room.

Her red-and-pink
dress is so pretty.

Next, she dresses up
as a pirate fairy!
Her hat has
a big white feather.

After dressing up,

Rosetta wants to

have a garden party.

Tinker Bell comes over
to help get ready.
The two friends
clean up Rosetta's room.

Tinker Bell and Rosetta
put on their dresses.

The other fairies come over.

They all look so pretty!

After the fairies
eat and drink,
they go outside
to the garden.

In the garden,
they laugh,
dance, and sing.

At night, the
fairies fly back
to their rooms.

They are sleepy

after a fun night.

The next day, the fairies get
together and thank Rosetta.
They tell Rosetta
she is special, too.

Rosetta smiles.
She loves her friends
and being a garden-
talent fairy.

Meet Silvermist

By Celeste Sisler

Attention, Disney Fairies fans!
Look for these words when you read
this story. Can you spot them all?

dress

frog

hat

boots

Silvermist is a water-talent fairy.

Her blue dress and pink
flowers are so pretty.

Silvermist lives inside
a drop of water.

She plays dress-up

with a frog in her room.

First, she puts on

a blue ball gown.

Next, Silvermist dresses up
as a pirate fairy.
She has an idea!

Silvermist flies fast
to Tinker Bell's room.
She tells Tink she will have
a pirate party today.

Tinker Bell thinks this is a good idea.

She helps Silvermist get ready

and puts on her pirate outfit.

The two fairies go to Zarina's room.

Zarina jumps with joy!

She will help with the party, too.

Each fairy's pirate outfit includes
a hat, a belt, a pair of boots,
and a hatpin for a sword.

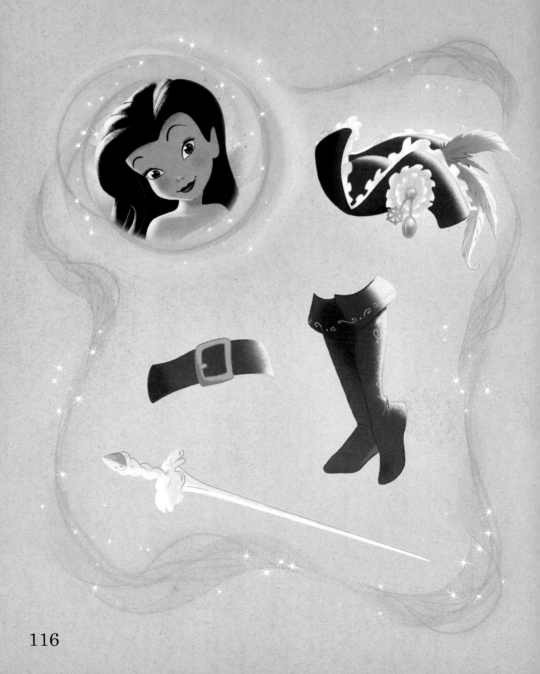

The three fairies fly to a pirate ship.

The other fairies meet them there.

Vidia, Iridessa, Fawn, and Rosetta
are in their pirate outfits.

Baby Crocodile is there, too!

When it is dark out,
the fairies go below the deck
and play games.

The next morning,
Silvermist brings her friends
to a waterfall.

She thanks them

for coming to her party.

She is so happy.

Her fairy friends are happy, too.
Silvermist made their day
bright and fun!

The End